The old Polish Legend

To commemorate 100 Years of Polish Independence

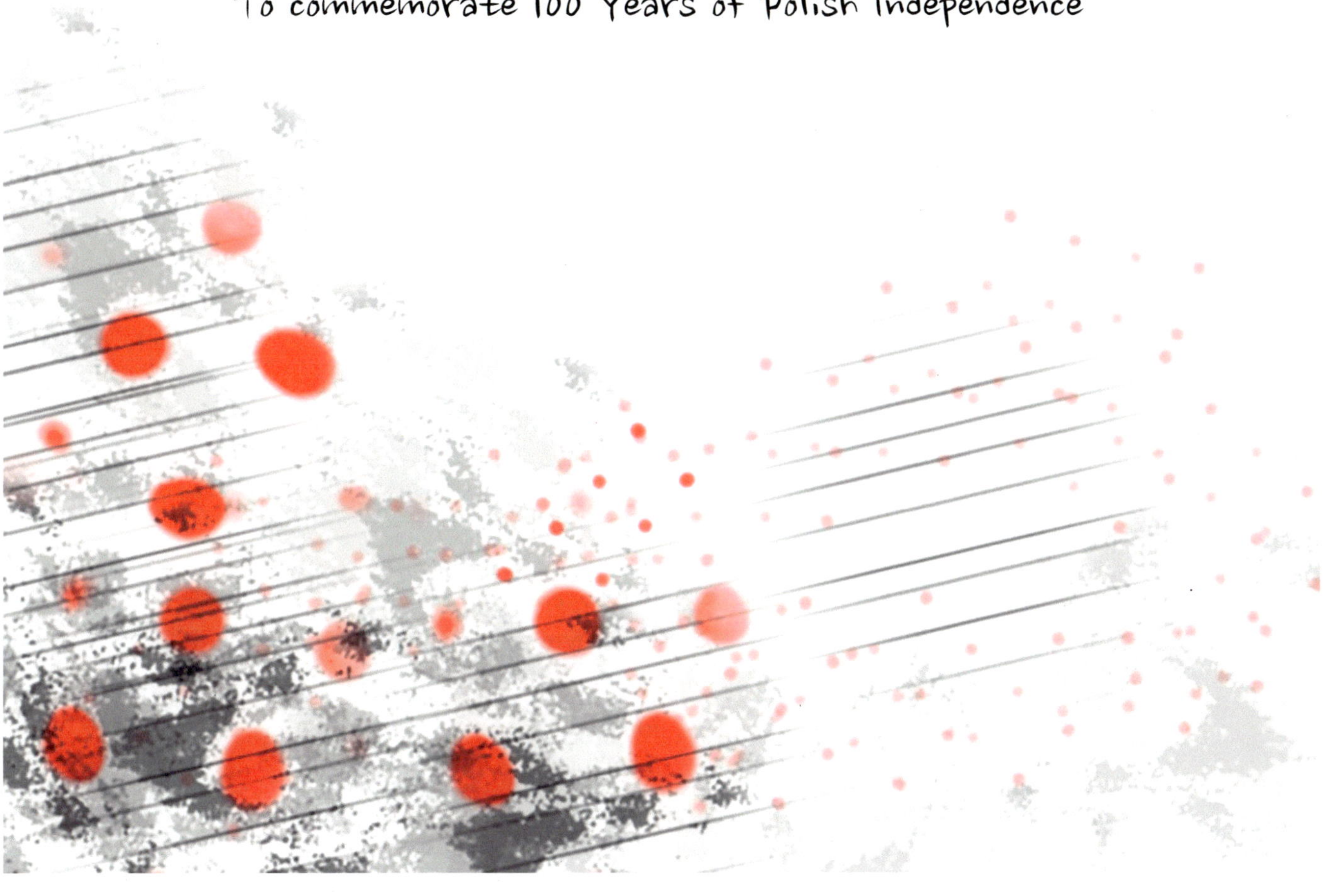

For Julia and Fabian and their friends....

Always look for a happy end!

P.S. Polish pronunciation can be tricky sometimes. To make sure your reading adventure is smooth and easy please say 'vavel' when you read the word **Wawel**. That means something along the lines of 'vavɛl', like ravel. Good luck!

First published in the United Kingdom in paperback in 2018

Text and illustrations copyright © 2018 by Justyna Majewska
Contact: www.justynamajewska.co.uk / justacreations@gmail.com

All rights reserved. No part of this publication may be reproduced, stored in a retrieval system, or transmitted in any form or by any means, electronic, mechanical, photocopying, recording or otherwise, without the prior permission of the author.

The Wawel Dragon

by Justyna Majewska

Here is a

story,

my little bro

which truly happened

a very long time ago

in a country

so brave and kind.

I'll tell you about it,

do you mind?

So, sit down and try to relax as I tell you some very important **facts!**

In the East there is a land

proudly named by the Slavic people as Poland.

Its winters are cold, summer months hotter.

There are mountains, lakes and the Vistula water.

It's emblem a white eagle standing guard

Right at the bottom to be exact

is a town built by big

King Krak

He ruled Krakow

for many good years

with just one thing

bringing him to tears.

In a grotto near the rising ground

the mysterious

Wawel Dragon

could be often found.

He was quite a big dangerous creature,

that would for sure scare your

favourite teacher.

His skin was green, teeth razor sharp. Constantly looking for apples, pheasants and **animals' hearts**.

The dragon was stealing local people's food leaving them hungry which was not so good.

Their only hope was some **brave knights**

who fought the dragon during long misty nights.

Unfortunately, the creature was massive and strong

And the ferocious battles took far too long.

You see, that wasn't a good solution.

Beating the indestructible

Dragon was just

an illusion!

But

one day

a very smart boy

had an idea to bring

back some joy!

He stuffed sheep with **a hot spice** mixed with nice red carrots and basmati rice.

Then he gave the tasty hot food

to the dragon who

growled

with a gratitude!

He ate the sheep without being suspicious and gave the impression that it was

delicious!

So, he rushed to the cold river

and drank gallons of water

making him shiver...

The dragon inflated like a gigantic balloon

and predictably, his body exploded

the same afternoon!

Our smart boy

was full of delight after killing the Wawel Dragon without a fight.

Finally,

the people of Krakow could celebrate Now their town is in a peaceful state!

Just to remember this time in history

The Krakovians built **a symbol** of their victory.

The dragon now stands on the hill

Go ahead and visit him— what a thrill!

Still quite big with teeth razor sharp

I hope his story has stolen

your heart!

THE END.

Keep an eye out for more Polish legends from justacreations!

Made in the USA
Monee, IL
21 December 2025

39695083R00017